The Awakening: Illumination

JD Williams

Copyright © 2012 Aphelion Press

ISBN: 0615697941
ISBN-13: 978-0615697949

This work of fiction is dedicated to all the men and women serving in the US Military. My brothers and sisters in arms are forever my inspiration.

CONTENTS

The Awakening: Illumination

PROLOGUE

The private diary of Eva Young

Monday January 26th
2156

I woke up late again today, as usual, but at least I wasn't late getting into work. My hair might not be "put together," like my boss wants, but at least I can show up on time, and my team is able to out produce everyone else here consistently for the past four years. Sure does put a frown on his face :-). Today is a new day they say. New beginnings and new opportunities the likes we have never seen or even imagined are supposed to make an appearance sometime later this afternoon. Whatever that means, as long as I don't have to stay late. I hate staying late.

Monday, January 26th
06:59

Waking up late wasn't the only snafu of that day. And that only happens when I drink the night before, though it's always one or two small mixed drinks. You'd think I was an alcoholic by the reaction I have. But I'm such a light weight it knocks me out almost instantly. For hours. Anyway, the hot water wasn't working again, and my door was stuck closed for the third time this week. I'm so thankful that the maintenance people are here so early, and are so eager to do their jobs. But this small loft apartment on the 324th floor of a modest building in the central district of New Chicago is a godsend. It's almost like the events of my life have been hand picked for me, each year carefully hand crafted to serve some specific purpose. I've been incredibly lucky! I'm only 25 (with a birthday coming up in three weeks!) but everything has fallen into place perfectly. But this entry isn't about that.

Dear diary, I hate my boss. I hate him so much it's almost sad. I don't dislike him, I don't just simply feel animosity towards him. I actually legitimately hate him. He gawks at me like I'm some piece of meat, gives me awkward shoulder rubs at the most inappropriate of times, and he's not even good looking. But today was the last straw. I can only be thankful for so much before I have to wonder why. Just why the hell are things going seemingly into the tubes? It's like overnight things have changed near completely.

He used to be such a nice guy, but ever since that night, he's been losing his hair and gaining weight, and presumably losing his mind along with his hair. It's like his personality is falling out of his head with the follicles of his hair. He's been at Abbott Laboratories for twenty five years, accounting for over 12 billion dollars of delicious revenue with the rest of us. Since before the war that changed everything. But he's wacko!

Anyway, I've gotta stay on topic here. He's an accountant, and I'm a certified professional accountant as well, leading a team of five other accountants in our mission to find wasteful spending and destroy it. We've saved over 358 million dollars, though we'll never see any of that in our pockets. But I've had a feeling for awhile that we've been cutting useless programs to make room for something else. I haven't told anyone my suspicions, but today I found a huge inconsistency in our budget forecasting. We're missing three billion dollars. Where the hell would something like that go?

I'm a little scared that something like that is going to end up on my shoulders now that I've seen it. I'll get blamed for such a wildly inaccurate issue. But that's not all. No no, that's just the beginning of the problems that cropped up today. I was digging, seeing where 3 billion dollars would go, where it would flow to, and I think I found the codename for a new project unlike any other. Project Themis (Seriously, what's with using ancient Greek words for these things, it's super cliché). That's all I can gather from looking the documents in the system, so tonight I'm going to do a little snooping around. I've never snuck into anything before, aside from my brothers room to steal the newest Aaron Allston novel. But breaking into quite possibly the most secure facility in the new world might prove fruitless. Where do I start? We only have one laboratory, occupying the same building I live in, but riding the speedy elevator down to the lower levels is a game I don't think I'm willing to play. The system can scan my skin temperature, retina and voice as I tell it where I want to go, and it takes all of that to determine just where have access. If you don't it doesn't let you, thankfully it won't like kill you right away or anything, but I wouldn't put such behaviors past my beloved company. Human trials have been happening here without us knowing for a long long time. Since before the war even.

11:23

I've been sitting here, twiddling my thumbs mindlessly trying to figure out what happened to my boss, and then it hit me. It was on the forefront of my mind all along. Human trials! Why is it that I'm so ditzy about such simple things? The most complex of problems flows so easily over my mind, with the solution popping into my head after mere milliseconds, but this was right in front of me! My mother always said I was special, I didn't really realize it meant the other kind of special too. Anyway, Glucerna, a 21st century wonder drink that helped diabetics enjoy nutritious and sweet libations has recently made a comeback in the hands of my immediate supervisor. I never noticed it until today, he's had a bottle of it nearly everyday for the past three weeks. Holy crap monkeys. Maybe this is a link in the chain of unfortunate events? Or maybe this is just another one of my wild paranoid theories where I make connections where there are none. Either way, it's the only change in his life, he's quite vocal and would have said something about added stress. Would have taken out that added stress on us. God I hate him.

Maybe I should be a writer or something? Anyway, Glucerna is our product, so maybe it contains something not kosher for human trials, something that has to be snuck into the mix to clandestinely test its effects. His complexion is a little ashen and lifeless now, with his hair almost completely gone. I hope he doesn't hear me recording this. Oh, shit, hold on.

11:28

That was close. I'll be recording more after tonights break in. I'll be scheduling an audit of resources to give myself a cover to get into the lab. Hopefully they'll buy it, and hopefully I can find something to satisfy my curiosity. This is just getting weird.

17:26

I'm on my way down to the sub basement floors to check out whats going on. I hope they buy this! I find it strange how this building is so incredibly tall, standing up by what seems like a thread of existence, but the elevator is so damn slow. It's also weird how the pharmaceutical companies took advantage of the large scale war that happened those long years ago. I'm not even old enough to remember, but the scars of war are still fresh in some parts of the world. Which is where Abbot Labs and other companies took the reigns from mankind to help with the recovery. I think Abbott branched off from pure medicinal drugs to creating solutions for terra-forming. Biological terra-forming. I think that's how Mars is being transformed. It's not quite complete yet though, but I think they created a catalyst that's been slowly but surely transforming the materials into something man livable. They also started programs geared towards soldiers, programs that helped regrow lost limbs and helped to heal the shattered minds of the brave. Even going so far as creating nano-viruses capable of destroying radiation sources and returning most of the world to a normal state. In our time of great need, the industry you'd think would do poorly or perhaps turn on humanity, actually saved it. Weird. That's another conspiracy theory for another time though.

I'm almost there, almost to the floor. This damn thing keeps stopping, and every time the door opens my heart skips a few beats. I always think that security can read my mind or something, and that they're one step ahead of me. Waiting and watching this whole time, behind the scenes biding their time until I make it obvious that I know. But I don't know. Oh, here I go. The final stop, Sub Level three, full of mysterious and disgusting things. If there really is a God, wish me luck!

17:46
"I like what I see, but what about this contraption here, what does this do and how much does it cost in upkeep,"

"Well Ma'am, this looks like an old bathtub, but is in fact a multi-sectioned horizontal cabinet incubator that we use to grow multiple strains of whatever we are working on. It's actually quite cheap to maintain, only requiring cleanings after each specific use and changing of some of the elements every six months or so. Since we manufacture this particular model, it comes out to about $600 a year give or take,"

"May I ask what the latest project inside there is,"

"Absolutely, it's called Pr........
static

17:59
"...mpressed with what you have, I see you've taken our suggestions to heart. Why don't you

get together with your staff and give me a list of costs associated to all the absolutely necessary equipment so I can further analyze what you ha...

static

18:06

"So what actually happens in this room then?"

"This room is actually where a new project is being developed, brainstormed really. Has to do with genetics and the like something like gene therapy to help those with terminal illnesses and such. It's quite the booming industry, especially now that we have the time and money to devote to such things. Hey, that door is locked for a reason, it's... messy in there, probably shouldn'...

static

19:25

I made it, I'm home and I made it. I tricked them and they bought it. I think I have the evidence I need, at least I have something that I can take somewhere. The room, the room that my guide said was locked, it had a weird odor coming from it, that and even though the window was tinted, I could make out what appeared to be a very large and spacious chamber. I couldn't make out much except some shiny lights and what looked like air ducts? Maybe? Round tube things going every which way. Anyway, the point is that I freaking got it!

Now some relax time with a glass of wine and a short nap before I head in to work tomorrow. I think I might like this investigative journalism stuff. Mayhaps I'll be able to finally change my career to something a little more exciting.

Tuesday, January 27th
01:34

I can't stand this felling that I feel deep inside. I know what they are doing. I just know it. Gene therapy? My ass it's just gene therapy. Jesus, I think they're literally attempting to change the genetic makeup of human beings. Like these sickos want to create something, awaken our primal past or whatever bullshit they sold the people in charge. They want to fucking genetically alter humans to their own god dammed design. I can't sleep, and the bottle of Pinot Blanc didn't help for shit. I have to tell someone. I have to. I have a headache and I can't sleep. Great. And I'm talking into my bed, and no one can hear me except this stupid microphone. Wait, what's that? Who's the...

static

Loud and sudden noises overheard in the background. "Holy shit. Holy shit. Holy shit. Holy shit. Get that fucking thing away from me! Don't you get any closer," Heavy breathing heard in the background. "God.... Dammit... Stop... this.... AHHHH!"

04:56

I still have the recording device in my pocket,

and it still appears to be getting a signal strong enough to back up away from here. I'm paralyzed, suspended in the air by something or other, and I can hardly even talk. I found what I was looking for. Human trials. They're testing on Humans for Christ's sake. Our greatest minds are trying to play God in the most ridiculous of ways, kind of *cough* like a, a weird cliché zombie film. This can't be happening. I dug too far too quickly and now they're going to do something to me! Help! If anyone hears this, please, help! 5th sub-level! PLEASE! HE..."

static

THE BEGINNING OF THE END

From the private journal of Christopher Wraith

This will be my final entry to this journal, if this is found, please, heed my warnings and take action to prevent what's to come. You are the only hope, if you fail to take action at this moment, then all of humanity is forever doomed.

Like so many other stories, this one starts quite simply from the beginning. This is how it began, how it happened, and how it will likely continue into the future. War, you see, is a terrible thing, terrible for all involved. It seems that the innocent and virgin mind can think of such events, such things happening and not understand at all the complexity of it all, the whys and wherefores that we kill each other. But once that virgin mind has been made an experienced and productive member of society, only then can they truly understand that they were right all along. It's not complicated, wars are created not because of the complicated political maneuverings that we see on television, but instead because of the simplistic animalistic instincts of someone who proclaims they "know" better in their attempt to lead societies and civilizations down paths that even they don't understand or know. But this isn't about the why, but the what and how. Why is for others to ponder and debate in sterile settings while the rest of us suffer due to the indiscretions and decisions they make. They being the leaders of our civilizations.

The year is 2156, and I was 21 years old, new, fresh, innocent and very much a virgin of even my own mind. But dates and my age are unimportant. Life was good, we were finally colonizing our moon and mars, exploring space as slowly as we could, and were generally not running out of resource anymore. Earth was as green, and grey, as ever. The debate and search for fossil fuels continued and persisted not unlike it did in the 21st century. But peace was had throughout the world. No, there wasn't a "One World Government" or some such nonsense, no huge socialist movement taking away the basic freedoms from the worlds masses. No, to have the diversity of our species and to live like civilized beings, we govern our own pockets of cultural diversity, separating things into independent states not unlike the United States of old, free to see to and govern their own. We were all united by our willingness to advance technologically and spiritually. We all faced a common enemy at this point, the threat of becoming extinct by our own hands. We as a species overcame that great hurdle, so it was another golden age for he Human Race. We were so full of hope, not to mention arrogance, that it was so easy to get lost and lose sight of the goal. But for a time we didn't. And that's where this journey begins. In 2156, the most foolish year of my life.

It wasn't foolish in the traditional meaning, no, I had my fair share of embarrassing misadventures whilst being educated about the finer points of college life. I have stood naked and drunk on a deck overlooking a metropolis while I yell obscenities. But it was a far more foolish year on a completely different level. You see, I wanted to be someone, I wanted to rise up into greatness and prove my worth on a physical and spiritual level. I wanted to be the equal of no one, able to make life saving or life taking decisions in less than a millisecond. I wanted to test my mettle against like minded individuals in the heat of battle, tasting sweat, blood and the dying screams of my adversaries as I hacked, cleaved and out-thought them one or a hundred at a time. And this was the year where I had even a modicum of gusto, or balls, to try to achieve this most reverent of dreams. But such things were silly fantasies of school children who took sides in wars that didn't exist anymore played out in video games and nothing more. Wars were practically an archaic idea, drawn out conflicts between nation states disappearing with the final battle of World War Three, finally setting our great world free, free to advance into the future of mankind, into this golden age. With that I was forced to do what I thought was the next best thing. I joined an organization determined to find life outside, or even inside, our solar system. I wanted to do something amazing, something that would be remembered by my children, my children's children, and for many generations to come. I wanted it, and I don't even know why. For some reason, I was compelled to be somebody, to be that person that was important not by general consensus, but instead because of my accomplishments. I was very much young, dumb, and blind to the world. Very much a virgin of existence yearning for my first experience. So I signed up for the non-profit organization that didn't have a name, or any real means to accomplish their mission statement.

There were a total of seven of us in this organization, all older than me, all male except one woman who was in charge of it all. She had set it up initially as a small pipe dream, an idea she wanted to expound upon over any years, and maybe convince young individuals such as myself to continue her work well after her demise. SETI revived so to speak. She was a professor, and I was her student and one point during my student "career," I was going through university not entirely sure what I wanted to specialize in, if anything, only thinking and dreaming of the great conflicts that I had just barely missed, but she enticed me with visions of adventure and excitement the likes of which I've never seen or even heard of. Her words were like a disease that slowly infected myself and the rest of the group with her wild ideas. She was charismatic and a natural leader, always positive and looking towards the future and the end goal. What young man wouldn't be interested in being on the forefront of discoveries that could very well change the course of the Human Race? She played on my boyish dreams of glory. I eventually gave in, with dreams of intergalactic war the likes of which I could only vaguely remember from a rather short and otherwise monotonous 21st century cinema course. Regardless, I was onboard with her idea now, a young man with a mission. All I wanted was purpose, and she gave it to me. Dr. Ann Haworth. It was only years later I would realize that were it possible to travel through time, that I would do it completely different. In short, it was a grave mistake. A mistake that may very well cost... Well I suppose that's actually for another time, for if you are reading this then perhaps you don't know yet, and it's best if you don't at the moment, as all will be revealed in due time. Ignorance, as they say, is indeed bliss.

The seven of us were not especially good friends, and were only united under the great purpose outlined and designed by Dr. Haworth, our great organizer and financier. In fact, we rarely interacted with each other save for when we were required to by our leader. Names, in this case, are largely unimportant, we should instead concentrate on the events described on these digital and paper pages. But we were united by the charismatic Dr. Haworth, moving forward in our dream and purpose to explore and find the very answers to life we all are curious about. Space exploration was a maturing industry, on the heels of new discoveries such as a means of faster than light travel, bending space time to our very will and forcing our way through the fabric of existence to another location. Using highly sensitive automated contraptions to see far into the depths of the universe, giving us a glimpse into the very beginnings of existence. But our natural curiosity didn't stop there. We were largely alone, believed to be an insignificant yet miraculous error, a statistically unlikely mutation that resulted in the planet we now call Earth. How could this be? How could we be so unique? No, in this golden age we aren't content to simply accept that we are alone, the sole heir to the throne of the universe. Religion has evolved just as much as we ourselves have, and we see the error in our ways. So we search. That is to say, that we seven take up the torch left by our ancestors of not so long ago and search the skies for the signs that we are not alone, and most importantly, that we are not insignificant. We were so unprepared.

The seven of us, brave explorers that we were, were about to undertake a journey of massive proportions, something the that would rival vision quests of Native American origins, and the whole journey of Buddhism itself. It would unravel the very foundations of our reality. And all this for what exactly? Dr. Haworth was quite the politician, able to secure contacts and equipment for our purposes. She swayed those that were in positions of importance and those who had the power to help us on our quest. Faster than light travel was only designed for inanimate objects, machines that were expendable if they happened to become lost in time or space. The effects on humans and other life have not been studied, but Dr. Haworth used her beguiling personality to secure the technology for our personal use. This was the first blunder.

For four years we set up apparatuses for recording the data sent back by satellites sent to the corners of the galaxy, as well as sifting through the historical material provided us by former employees of the long extinct SETI institute. We stayed up many long nights simply staring at screens, double checking the computer analysis hoping for some sign of anything. Weeks without sleep as we were driven nearly mad by our master as if we were nothing more than her slaves. She had absolutely no regard for our personal lives, assuming quite vehemently that we were dedicated solely to her cause. Her eyes, though, were empty and lifeless. Perhaps her search was internal, a search for her own soul expressed through the external. It was as if she were missing, replaced by an automaton blindly leading the masses to our doom. But we followed. We followed her every word, almost unquestionably. She had us firmly in her grasp, and this was our second mistake. We were blind, blind to her true nature, blind to the nature of what she wanted to accomplish.

It was a rather unremarkable spring day, not too cold nor too warm. A slight breeze swirled around the courtyard outside the entrance to our research center in Colorado Springs, CO. It was early in the morning and I had yet to enjoy my first delicious cup of coffee. But this unremarkable day in spring was soon to be one of the most extraordinary day in the history of human kind. Dr. Haworth and my colleagues were not there, as usual they were off running errands, perhaps running to Starbucks or something similar. But whilst I was booting up my personal computing machine, a peculiar noise erupted from the room next door, the room where the computational equipment just happened to be analyzing recently downloaded data from a deep space probe sent to Kepler-11 in recognition of it's significance to the failed Kepler project of the early 21st Century. You see, Kepler-11 is some 2000 light-years away, and thus we can only "see" the early development of such a star and it's corresponding extra-solar planets. So therefore we were wrong, very wrong to simply cancel any remaining research efforts. For on this unremarkable spring day, we finally detected the presence of life elsewhere in the galaxy. We were finally not alone. The data that the computers were analyzing was electromagnetic in nature, and related to frequencies that are common to humans, similar to the SETI of old, but on a local planetary scale. I nearly passed out as I entered our server room. And this was no error, because the accuracy of the algorithms that we created to search was incredible. We had done it, we had changed the course of history forever. But what would it mean? This discovery, was our third mistake.

Life was finally visible in Dr. Haworth's eyes. She said she felt young again, like a child who had just found out how to crawl. It was utterly remarkable. This, however, was just the beginning, and would subsequently be the easiest part of this discovery. The life that now shown brightly from within Dr. Haworth's eyes re-invigorated her, re-lit the flame that had burned so brightly before. We were finally on our way. A mere four months after the discovery of this signal we were able to translate the underlying broadcast from it's native language, of which it was nothing more than a broadcast that leaked into space, slowly losing it's energy until we caught it. After this, though, events seemed to move a little more swiftly. Three weeks later we were boarding an experimental craft designed more for cargo than humans, and after nearly a month of flying near blind through the cosmos, our team finally arrived. We had flown 2000 light-years to discover a new species, hopefully somewhat like our own. The vista was beautiful! It was absolutely magnificent. The star itself, appearing before us like hell itself, with solar flares bursting from it in all directions near constantly, irradiating us with heat, light and x-ray's, more than the ship could handle. But we persisted. It had been a very long month in the darkness of deep space and we were exhausted.

Within minutes we were pointed towards the aphelion of the third planet, speeding towards a majestic blue-green orb that could have been mistaken for Earth itself. It was exciting, the butterflies and anxiety making rounds among us. Dr. Haworth pulled us aside and gave us a rousing pep-talk, raising our spirits and once again uniting us in our common goal of discovery. She reminded us that it was indeed a rare experience and we could only be so lucky as to be there on that glorious day.

Luck, however, was not with us on that day. We approached the planetoid quickly, but as we approached something quite peculiar struck our eyes. The lush blue-green orb faded to a dull grey-brown and the orbit slowed, as if it were dying right before us. But it did not do as you may think. No, it did not explode in a spectacular display unlike any other we have witnessed, no, instead it simply became dark and lifeless. The oceans that were, seconds ago, shimmering brightly from the reflected rays of the systems star became dry. Was this some sort of trick? A hoax? A lie perhaps, engineered by the great Dr. Haworth? But for what? Why? Regardless, we remained on the approach, determined to find the source of our precious signal.

Two excruciatingly long hours passed before the fruits of our labors were realized. The originator of the signal that we processed and analyzed and spent billions of Dollars and thousands of man hours pursuing was finally found.

This is where the story ends and the present begins again. We were attacked viciously, Dr. Haworth led us into a trap. She squealed with delight as we flew towards our doom. She mysteriously disappeared during the barrage that followed, a barrage that tore us apart like we were but a piece of paper. It was horrific, four of the remaining six were disintegrated in the initial salvo. They anticipated us, this race of beings drew us here in order to destroy us. This is only the beginning and I can only imagine the horrors they want to bring upon the Human Race.

But I am alive still, for now. Just a few hours ago we crashed onto this planet, twisting and tumbling through gorgeous ruined spherical skyscrapers that seemed to hover above the ground. Us two, the remaining brave explorers are running for our lives, praying to every deity imagined that we were undetected, that they made an error in their own judgment and assume us for dead. Or perhaps they know we won't survive in this irradiated wasteland. I have recorded this journal in hopes that this will serve as a warning for Earth, or at least for other species as they are lured here like we were.

"Jan! Don't go in... Dammit, we have to keep going, Hey, Jan! God Dammit! Look out!"
Static

AWAKE

He awoke with a gasp in what felt like a foreign land, disoriented and confused. Pain radiated from the back of his head as if he'd been slammed in the back of the head with a sledge hammer. He struggled to open his eyes and noticed only a blur of light shining through from beyond. What the hell is this he thought, where the hell am I? The darkness covering him felt heavy and oppressive on his body, and the stench of death wafted into his nostrils. He tried to scream out, but his mouth was too dry to make anything more than a harsh rasping noise.

A short distance away a terrifying guttural and hungry howl broke his concentration, sending his thoughts spiraling towards the unlimited possibilities. He was paralyzed with fright at the sound, so much so that it shook him to his very core. The howling in the distance was repeated again and again for several horrible moments that seemed to last forever.

Jesus Christ! He thought as he lay waiting for what he thought could very well be his end.

The howls continued for what seemed like an eternity, but thankfully were slowly fading off into the distance. When they could no longer be heard, he decided to attempt moving again. He can't possibly be dead, the intense pain radiating from the back of his head is testament to that, you don't feel pain when your dead, right? Moving his arms and legs proved an almost fruitless venture, the weight of the darkness covering him was severely limiting, not to mention the pain the back of his head flared intensely with every attempted movement.

Over the next several long tedious moments he was able to slowly wiggle his way through a small break in the darkness, using nothing but pure desperation to free an arm and using that newfound leverage to help roll the dark heavy mass off of him. That "mass" of darkness fell away with a hollow thunk, and it was only then that he realized that the darkness on top of him was actually the bloody mutilated corpses of something that only vaguely resembled human bodies. With wide cautious and fearful eyes he slowly lifted himself out and away from the bodies, struggling to gain his balance with his tired muscles. When the man stood up, he quickly rubbed the back of his head to try to soothe the pain he still felt. Thankfully, there was no obvious wound there.

When he looked around to survey his surroundings, he didn't recognize anything. The rocky barren landscape was covered in a dusty red haze, and the terrain was highlighted by the harsh blue glow of the sun. Small, ground hugging, spiny looking shrubs dotted the ground in wild looking patterns. To the West was a canyon with what looked like remnants of a dried up river twisting through the center of it. To the East was jagged rocky, dangerous looking terrain for as far as the eye could see. To the North were plains studded with tall stalagmite looking protrusions thrusting up from the ground almost angrily to the sky. And to the south was a short walk to a steep cliff leading off into who knows where. There was not a single sign of civilization in sight, nothing at all to indicate where he might be. This was starting to become more terrifying by the moment, with the thought of rescue slipping further and further from his mind.

Out of instinct he yelled at the top of his lungs for help, "Help! Anyone!" He didn't expect anyone to hear him at this point. His thoughts were wandering very close to the fact that he might die on this alien landscape. Before he could lose too much hope he took his first step in a vain attempt towards finding his way home.

The mystery man chose to follow the sun as it was setting into the vast valley to the West. Maybe that dried up river will lead the way to civilization. As he started his journey, a wind started to blow towards him, as if trying to warn him. And with that wind, he thought he heard something vaguely familiar, as if it were speaking to him.

"Aalllennn," it seemed to whisper. "Aalllennn,"

* * * * *

She sat by the bedside in a dimly lit room in Legacy Emanuel Hospital in Portland, OR, quietly holding his hand as he lay there almost lifeless in a coma on the bed. Occasionally she would glance up from where she was staring off and whispered into his ear.

"Allen, I love you, please come back, I need you, we need you," She had been here at the hospital by his side for the past two days faithfully by his side. Emily never expected to be a widow at such a young age, and wasn't going to let that happen just yet. Their unborn child was going to have a father regardless of what fate thought. They had had a wonderful life together, and the past two days Emily was thinking about all the amazing times they had together, the short life they lived together. It was just last summer that they went on a cruise to Alaska to see the first artificial birth of a North Pacific Right Whale, a magnificent event that helped them both to realize that they too wanted to be parents one day. Her thoughts were interrupted when the doctor, Dr. Walker, knocked on the door.

"May I come in?"

"Of course," Emily replied softly. Dr. Walker walked up to her and put his hand on her shoulder.

"How're you holding up today Em?"

"I'm doing ok, as well as can be expected I guess," She continued to stare at Allen's hand she was holding. Not willing to look up from it for even a second.

"Well, Em, I've got some good and some bad news about Allen. Do you want to start with the good, or the bad first?"

"Let's start with the bad, better to leave here on a good note."

"Ok, well, this is hard to say, but I suppose that I have to," Dr. Walker clearly didn't want to say this, sweat was beginning to form on his forehead, and he was fidgeting with his hands.

"His, um, well, his outlook doesn't really look too good at this point. The damage to his parietal and occipital lobes is just too great. If he does recover on his own it could take many many years,"

Emily was trying to hold in her emotions, but it was inevitable and a few tears escaped on to her cheek. She didn't quite know how to respond to that. The news was too much to bear at that moment. Her husband, her best friend, and ultimately her soul mate could be lost forever. It took a few moments for her to recover from the shock of that last statement, and thankfully Dr. Walker was kind enough to let her be. He just stood behind her patiently waiting and lightly rubbing her back to help soothe her.

"Wait," She finally replied, her voice quivering.
"What do you mean, on his own? What does that mean?" Dr. Walker had a half crooked smile as he was asked this, he was holding in a lot of excitement about what he had to say next.

"Well, that's the good news. There is something we can do, something very experimental, and because of that, it's also very expensive."

"Bu-" Emily started to say, but was swiftly cut off by the excited doctor.

"However, there is a way to have this done for free, sort of," Emily finally released her husbands hand and turned around to look suspiciously up at the doctor. She wiped tears and running makeup from her eyes.

"Stem-cells," The Doctor said. "We can use stem-cells to help regenerate and repair the damage. There's some much improved technique. It's safe and effective. Listen, I'll leave you here to think about it, we can discuss the details later. It does involve a contract of sorts though. But just so you know, I think it's a great deal, and you should definitely take it,"

As Dr. Walker turned to walk out of the room he turned to say "I think you have an idea what those details are, chance of a lifetime ya know,"

Emily put her hands to her face and started to sob.

* * * * *

With the blue sun setting behind him and darkness was beginning to set in and there was no moon to light his way. The dusty wind had turned chilly as the sun disappeared. Allen had been walking along the canyon for what seemed like hours. His white linen short sleeved button up shirt, khaki pants and black boots were covered in a fine red powder thanks to the non stop gusting winds of this dreary place. The howling creatures that still haunted his mind haven't been heard since he first woke up, giving him a false sense of security. He was cold, dirty, and incredibly thirsty, and still wondering what the hell this place really was. Nothing made sense here, nothing at all. He was still thinking about the whispering voice that sang so sweetly in his ears as if on the wind itself. It sounded so familiar familiar, it sounded more than familiar, like it was a part of him somehow. He wished he could recall what that voice meant to him, see a face, maybe even put just a name to it. But alas, all he could do was wonder. That, and continue walking.

His feet ached, he was ravenously hungry, and he smelled rank. He was so famished that he even considered eating a non-vital organ or something just to regain a small amount of energy. Why couldn't he remember anything? Had he suffered a blow to the head? The aching bloody mess on the back of his head pointed to that fact, but you'd think he'd be able to remember something important or useful. It seemed like he had just been born, thrust from the primordial goo into an already active and very violent world, with no recollection as to who or even what he is. Thoughts, namely flashes of far away feelings stung at him inside his mind, as if fire ants were attempting to burrow into his mind carrying his memories. But he was unable to hold on to them, unable to recognize anything. He was lost in an alien world that at the same time felt oddly familiar. He gazed off into the distance, surveying the barren gritty landscape beyond. The ashen spiny undergrowth seemed to sway in the light breeze that took shape, dust and sand swirling about in a maelstrom of despair, deepening his sense own sense of desperation. It seemed easy simply walk in circles for days out here with nothing at all resembling life in sight. A burning desire, for survival, for something, he didn't know, could be felt in the back of his mind, almost quite literally on the back of his head. So he wandered, and continued wearily into the darkness.

Off in the distance through the darkness he spotted an overhang on the side of the canyon that looked large enough to use as a shelter. With hope still wavering, he continued on. After too many minutes and too many steps, he finally arrived at the overhang, which was more shallow than he had hoped. He began to shiver, so decided to try to uproot a few of the spiny bushes to see if they were edible or to use as tinder to make a fire, but in the end they got the best of him and ended up hurting his hands enough to draw blood. With that, he gave up on making a fire and decided it would be best to simply retire for the night. Sleep would hopefully give him enough strength to get him out of this mess in the morning. Maybe this is a dream. He thought. Maybe I'll wake up at home, where ever the hell that is, and this will just be some kind of sick and twisted nightmare. Although it certainly felt real enough, but aren't dreams supposed to feel real? Hope, that's all he could do as he laid himself down under the overhang and tried to make himself comfortable. At least it's peaceful here. He mused. The sound of the wind should be soothing enough to help him to sleep.

A rustling in the distance woke him up slowly. He propped himself up on an elbow unsteadily as he waited for his faculties to wake up from their less than blissful slumber. The rustling was joined by a fast, heavy and harsh breathing sound. It's too dark to see anything, but the breathing sounds as if it's getting closer, the creature he can imagine inching it's way along, saliva dripping off of sharp fangs, ready to feast on his weakened body. Furious, but tired, he sits up, closes his eyes and pounds his fists into the ground. "Ahhhh!" He screamed to no one in particular, if only to block out the horrible sounds making their way ever closer to him. "This can't be happening! God dammit!" he exclaimed, while continuing to pound his fists into the hard soil at his side.

* * * * *

She tossed and turned as the night went on, throwing pillows and blankets away as she did so. Emily was having the nightmare again, in stunningly good detail. The sweat was running off of the forehead of the gunman, the shaking of his hands and the unsteady eagerness of his words.

"Get the fuck back! Don't you come any closer or I'll blow your brains out!" The gunman, one of three that fateful day at the Columbia Credit

Union robbery that might still prove to take her husband, was the youngest of the three, too young to be committing acts of violence like this. The world was supposedly a better more fair place these days. But regardless of how the kid came to be in the company of his thieving friends, the fact remained that the was in control of the fate of someone very dear to Emily's heart.

"Easy now fella, I just want to talk, I swear I won't be trying anything," Allen held his hands in front of him to show his palms in a gesture of goodwill.

"I just want to see if we can work something out. Now who's the guy in charge here?" The kid looked increasingly nervous now, his eyes moving left and right.

"It's Ji.. Wait a minute, I ain't gonna give up no names! You just tried to trick me!" The frightened boy lifted his hand like he was going to pistol whip Allen. He had every right to be nervous, everyone else in the Credit Union was sitting down on their hands, making only the occasional whimper. He hadn't expected anyone to be confrontational, it definitely wasn't in the plan they rehearsed. They were supposed to walk in during broad daylight, demand the money and run. It wouldn't be expected, no one robbed a bank that way anymore, it was too stupid an idea! But that's why it was supposed to work.

"Just let him talk, you keep your eye on him and the rest of the folk, and I'll occupy him while he finishes," The husky voice appeared from behind Allen, complete with another gun aimed at him. "I take it that you may just happen to be in charge then, so let's talk this out, no one needs to get hurt here ya know,"

"I decide that, and if I feel like killing today, then by God I'll kill someone! If it weren't for this stupid one government bullshit taking what's rightfully ours we wouldn't need to be doing this anyway,"

"Hey now, I'm not who you're angry at, maybe we can find a solution. Like asking nicely for the cash, maybe smiling a little bit," The attempt at humor was supposed to disarm the man, if only slightly, but it only did the opposite. The husky voiced man's eyes bulged with rage at the comment. Clearly he didn't think it as funny as Allen did. "All I'm saying is just put the guns down, no need to point them at us if we don't pose a threat, we don't need a trigger happy young kid making a mistake of his lifetime,"

The husky voiced man nodded ever so slightly to his young partner behind Allen, and then the relative silence was broken with a Bang! As the kid shot his pistol at the line of people near the front counter. Screaming erupted from the crowd as an older woman, innocent in all of this, fell over onto the floor gurgling as her lungs filled with blood from the gunshot. "Quiet!" The husky voiced man yelled. "There'll be plenty more of that if you keep it up mister, so sit the fuck down and shut up!"

Allen stared on in horror, completely stunned at what he saw. A completely unprovoked act of violence directed towards a innocent person. No one deserved to die today, for any reason. All they had to do was take the money and leave, but instead they took their time and seemed to actually enjoy terrorizing the unfortunate people who thought today was going to be a good day to go to the bank. "Whoa Whoa Whoa!" Allen yelled as he crept closer to the supposed leader, still showing the palms of his hands. "You didn't have to do that! We were co-operating, giving you everything you wanted!"

The masked husky voiced man just stared at Allen, with the outlines of a smirk forming on his mask.

"Terror causes change you idiot, didn't you pay attention over the last few decades? We're taking the money, a few lives, and that'll turn the wheels of change!" With that, Allen knew that negotiation was beyond his power, that this man and the group he represented absolutely did not want to discuss their philosophy, or be convinced there was another way. There was only one solution to this problem, and only one chance to take it. Thankfully the husky voiced man had a flair for the dramatic, and was still talking about how he planned to change the world, waving his gun around in the air as he did so, raising his voice as if he were playing the part of a villain in a movie. It was almost comical, but that was feeling was drowned out by the older woman laying in a pool of her own blood on the ground. If he didn't take this chance he would regret it, and feel terrible for the rest of his life. This man was most likely to take another life today, and Allen wasn't about to let that happen.

As the husky man continued his monologue, unaware of his surroundings, Allen slowly inched closer and closer. This was almost too easy. The other masked man was distracted by the emotional speech his boss was giving, probably shedding a tear as well. With both of the intruders distracted and the third still struggling with the security measures in place in the Credit Union, Allen started moving more quickly toward the leader, his back was turned, and his gun out in front of him waving wildly as he spoke about something to do with the atrocities of the modern world. Allen knew this was it, he felt it. Allen took a few leaping steps then lunged at the leader, wrapping his arms around him and trying to control his gun arm. They both tumbled to the ground with a loud Thud with Allen on top. All he needed to do was wrestle the gun from him and this situation would dissolve within seconds.

Bang! The sound ringed in his ears as his body suddenly fell limp, numb. He couldn't feel anything, couldn't scream, and could only wonder what had gone wrong as his world faded to black. And then nothing...

Emily woke up gasping for air. She was sweating profusely and breathing hard. She sat up in bed, with tears slowly forming the corners of her eyes. She felt around for and turned on the lamp next to her bed. She couldn't hold back the tears anymore and they started to pour as she sobbed. She wasn't there when it happened, but her mind kept re-constructing the events as they were described in the police report. She wished she hadn't read it.

* * * * *

The creature had slowly made its way over to where the man was pounding his fists into the ground. Breathing quickly and with a harsh rasping noise. The creature hunched over before him smelled of death, and had saliva and what looked like fresh blood dripping from the jagged sharp fangs of its open mouth. The reptilian creature stood at least six feet tall on two large reverse articulating legs with 3 large talons, two in the front and one in the rear. The saurian had grimy dark red scales along its body that looked touch enough to protect it from anything short of a firearm. The creature stuck its forked tongue out from its flat lipless face to taste the fear emanating from the man in front of him. The creature cocked his head in a gesture that looked of curious hunger. The man could feel the its warm breath on his face, could see the eerie glow of its eyes in the darkness, staring deep into his soul. Frozen in fear, the man could only stare back, wondering when the end was going to come. He had been close to death once already since he'd arrived in this world, and the second time wasn't any easier. "What do you want!" The man cried out.

The creature's forked tongue tasted the fear in the air. "The darkness will prevail, there is no where to go," It said with broken English. The creature then reached out a clawed hand slowly and pressed his four fingered hand against the mans chest, as if to feel his heartbeat. With a swipe, the saurian creature tore into his chest with his four short claws, tearing his shirt and drawing blood. The man still couldn't move. The creature took is hand and reared it back as if to strike again, but this time at his face, and the man clumsily scampered backwards in an attempt to escape the darkness before him. That attempt was futile, and he knew it. If this thing before him wanted him dead, than he would be dead no matter what he did to try to prevent it. He moved backwards, using his hands to pull himself, and kicking with his legs as fast as he could manage. His progress was stopped short as he ran into the wall behind him. The end of the line for me. He thought. He struggled to stand up as the creature was nearing him, still slowly, which confused him. He put his hand on the wall behind him, not even looking at it, to help steady himself as he stood up and ended up falling over a ledge. Splash!

He hit the water hard, headfirst. It must have been at least a 20 meter drop. This was certainly unexpected. He thought he had explored the overhang, it wasn't very deep at all, there wasn't anything else aside from a slightly curving rock wall. Where had this come from? How had he missed it? He was tired, but he didn't think he was that tired. The beady eye slits of the reptile were peering over the ledge at him, the forked tongue slicing the air rapidly, tasting the fear and confusion of his prey. Without skipping a beat, the man sank lower in the water, and swam in the only direction available, down a long dark winding tunnel going to who knows where. His chest stinging where he was clawed and his blood clouding the water behind him as he swam.

Harder and harder he swam, the pain in his chest turning to numbness as he continued through the maze of tunnels, swimming harder and harder trying to concentrate on the task at hand. But it was impossible, even as his bodily and mental functions were slowly shutting down as he was running out of oxygen, the image of the beast in the cave was freshly etched into his mind. The underground waterways seemed to go on forever, twisting and turning for what seemed like miles to him. Just as he was losing feeling in his body as was edging closer to blacking out, he saw ahead of him a stream of light beaming down from above, lighting the tunnel with hope.

With a gasp he broke through the surface of the water then wildly and blindly grasped for anything in reach to help him up. His hands found purchase on a small ledge a short distance above the water, and he hung there, exhausted, breathing heavy and thankful for every single breath. Pulling himself over the ridge proved to be quite the task, taking more energy than he had. But he prevailed and threw himself over the ledge with a giant heave. After several long seconds lying on the ground, he picked himself up by the elbows and surveyed his surroundings. Beyond the ledge was an immense cave that was lit by the bioluminescent glow being cast by small creatures attached to the walls. The ceiling was obscured by clouds that had formed from the moisture of the tall tropical trees and vegetation covering the basin of the enormous cavern. The site was both stunning and daunting at the same time.

What the hell is happening! The man sat down cross-legged, his head resting on his hands in his lap. Thinking. Alllennn. There it was again, the voice being carried by the wind, almost beckoning him. For a singular moment, he almost remember who he was, almost remember something very important, but he couldn't quite catch the thought as it flew into and then out of his head again. Please! Allennn! He started shaking his head back and forth as tears formed at the corner of his eyes. He was lost, alone, and completely without hope. "Please!" He pleaded. But no one was there to listen. In the distance the jungle was disturbed and avian wildlife was scattering quickly. Out of the wood-line a human shaped figure was seen running towards him. Rapidly.

DISCOVERY

"How're you doing Rosa?" Emily entered her favorite patient's, Rosa's, room. She had been at the hospital battling small cell lung cancer for 15 years now. Emily had "inherited" her when she started her residency. Despite the challenges Rosa has been through, she still maintained an incredibly positive attitude that was a testament to her strength of character. And today was even more reason to remain positive. She was finally in remission, and the outlook was looking very good. "Oh, I'm fine dear, just fine. What's for breakfast? Same old same old?" Although the food was above average, the breakfast items weren't anything special. But today, Emily had snuck into the kitchen early in the morning to cook up something special for a special day. Emily brought the pewter dish from around her back and into view. "Today we have a three egg omelet with spinach, cheddar cheese and a little sour crème on top," Rosa's eyes lit up at the sight of the delicious cuisine.

"I didn't know you could cook!"

"I'll take that as a thank you," Emily smiled. She knew she meant well, and probably was mostly unaware of the pain she was feeling with Allen being in a coma. Rosa did have her own problems to worry about of course.

"You know, young lady, you've been looking awfully tired as of late. Are you alright? Pregnant?"

"No, no, I'm not pregnant. Yet anyway. I've had a lot on my mind lately, work stuff ya know," She wasn't about to ruin her day with sad news.

"It's not healthy you know. Just look at those bags under your eyes! You need your beauty rest!"

"I know, thank you, I'll see what my boss will let me do today. I could use a good nap,"

"Tell him I said you can take a three hour nap!"

"Well, enjoy the good day, looks like it'll be sunny outside as well today," She walked over to open the blinds so she could enjoy the warm sun through the window. Not quite the same as actually feeling it on your skin, but good enough considering. Emily walked out whistling a happy tune. Seeing Rosa always cheered her up. Maybe she can take a nap today, if it's not too busy of course.

Ring Ring! Emily's phone rang a classic almost ancient ringing tune while she was walking out of her last patient's room. Oh no, I can't be taking any calls today. She thought. If she was going to get through the day and get on with life she would need a little more peace and quiet than this. It was already 10 o'clock in the morning and she had already had two people come into the emergency room from separate car crashes already in a coma, bringing to the forefront of her mind the pain she was desperately trying to hide. Her job was stressful enough on its own, she didn't need this. Oh look, it's "Bob," great.

"Dr. Walsh speaking, how may I help you?" Listening to his voice was almost as bad as drinking a vial of poison. He was a shady character, that was for sure. But aside from that, he just seemed like a terrible person, regardless of his "intentions" to help.

"Why hello there Em, how have you been?"

"It's Doctor Walsh, and I've been fine, and very busy at work, meaning I'm short on time,"

"Well, this'll be short. Have you had time to talk to your colleague about the little offer we've extended?"

"Oh yes, I've considered it, and I don't think that I'm quite ready to make a decision as of yet, so do me a favor and stop calling me. I'm not ready to move on and make a decision like that yet. It's too hard for me right now. In fact, I'm gonna go now. I'm about ready to throw this phone against the wall, and I've got two patients that need immediate attention,"
"We'll call you back in a couple—" Bob was cut short as Emily slammed the call end button with her palm. She squeezed her phone with rage before taking a deep breath to calm down/ This wasn't easy, and this "Bob" guy wasn't making anything any easier. She wasn't ready to move on at all. She didn't want to move on. This was all happening so fast for her. Dammit why!

"Back to the rat race I guess," She pushed open the doors leading into the emergency room and walked in and expelled a huge sigh. It was going to be a long rest of the day.

* * * * *

The shadow moved faster and faster towards the lone man. The man stands up, puts his hands over his eyes and screams as loud as his lungs will allow. "Ahhhhhh! LEAVE ME ALONE! I

CAN'T TAKE THIS ANYMORE!" his ear splitting scream didn't seem to have an effect as the shadow figure leaped up the small incline to where he was standing. Some of the bioluminescent creatures crawled along the walls close by to reveal the features of the shadow.

The man put his hands out in front of him, showing he meant absolutely no harm. Not that he was much good in a fight, as tired as he was. As the shadow stepped closer revealing even more of it's features, the man became shocked. This humanoid was familiar somehow, but he couldn't quite remember who or what he was. It was on the edge of his memory, what was left of it at least, and just wouldn't reveal itself.

"Hello there," The shadow said.

"It's ok, I just have something I want to tell you, I'm not going to hurt you, I promise," The voice was familiar, comforting even. Who was this guy?

"I'm glad you're alive, we've got a lot to talk about, and even more to do before going back. So follow me, I've got a place to sit down, some water, and some really delicious food," Without thinking, and trusting his instincts, the lone confused man followed the humanoid down the small slope into the heart of the cave, coming to a well travelled path that led into the jungle. They walked quickly, as if they were being followed, and without any conversation. The man was curious who this other man was. Maybe he had answers to offer, maybe he had a way out. He did say something about "before you go back," That in and of itself sounded like good news. The path they followed was relatively easy, winding through the jungle in large and long esses. It seemed as if hours had passed when the other man finally said something. "We're almost there, just a few more minutes and I can tell you what I've got. Oh, and relax by the way, you're not dead,"

"Wait, who said that I was dead?" The unknown man said confusedly.

"No one, silly head. Just letting ya know in case you were wondering. Now hurry up!" Oh my, maybe he's just telling me I'm not dead to make me feel better? Because this is some kind of after life meaning it's still life? Dammit! A thousand different possibilities were racing through his mind, almost as fast as his heart was racing. Ahead of them looked like a wall of vegetation, impassible without a machete or flame-thrower, but the shadow of a man walked through it as if it didn't exist.

"Wait!" The mystery man said, realizing it was too late. He took a deep breath, held it, then took a running start into the vegetation, only to emerge on the other side and lose his balance. He fell to the ground hard and rolled once to land on his face in front of the shadowed figure.

"Trust me," He said "I'm not going to let anything happen to you. Haven't ever, won't now,"

"Ughh," The man remained face down for some time before finally getting the strength to get himself up. It'd be so much easier to just stay down like this with my eyes closed letting the world pass me by. The shadowed figure was sitting down and motioned for him to come join him. Reluctantly, the man slowly walked over to the mossy log being used as a seat.

"I'd rather stand, if you don't mind. I don't exactly trust you yet,"

"Fair enough," The shadow responded.

"So just who the hell are you, and what they hell is this. I'm getting very annoyed with all of this, so you better have one dammed good explanation,"

"You'd better sit down, don't want you falling down again. This is going to be quite the unbelievable story," The shadowy figure motioned again for the log, smiling and patting the wet moss next to him.

"Thanks, but I'll still stand," With that, he folded his arms in front of him, and glared at the shadow with intense curiosity and skepticism. Whatever he had to say, he was sure he wasn't going to like it.

"Allen, it's me Mike, I know you probably don't have much of a memory right now and don't recognize me very well, I didn't remember much when I first woke up, but you can trust me, it'll all come back to you shortly. We've been friends for nearly a decade now, and I would never lie to you. Now listen, I have no idea where we are, but we're on another planet, probably some sick game reserve because I've been chased by nasty creatures ever since I woke up. But regardless, we found each other and now we can make it out of here. Steal a ship or something. So no, you aren't dead, not by a long shot,"

The mystery man's face was white, his arms had dropped to his sides and he was shaking. It was all too much to take in.

"I, I have to sit down," He stumbled over to the log and sat down, missing the log entirely and slamming softly onto the ground below. "What the- but-" He was speechless and confused. What this Mike character was saying to him didn't make any sense, and didn't clear up any of the thoughts racing through his mind. In fact, it just made things worse. He sat on the ground, back against the log, knees in his chest, shivering and staring off into the ground, the surreal ground of another planet, probably far from Earth, far from home. He sat and thought to himself, wondering furiously what this all was.

For all he knew, he was just some insane child living out a fantasy in his own mind. Mike kneeled down and slowly put his hand on his shoulder, in a vain attempt to try to comfort him.

"It's going to be ok," Mike said, trying to convince himself as well.

"You're name is Allen, and we'll figure this one out together. Just like all those adventures we went on when we were younger, right?"

PROGRESS

Emily smiled and laughed. "Oh you, that's not funny!" Her friend, Zoe, was telling a story about accidentally tripping a kid while she was in a shopping daze the other day. Emily was having brunch with a few of her close friends from work outside of a coffee shop near the hospital. A well deserved reprieve from the last 24 hours of torture at the hands of the hospital management.

"And then the poor little guy just lied there, face down in the floor not moving! I thought for sure he as dead! But then his Mother came over and apologized for his rambunctious behavior, telling me he got what he deserved!"

"Zoe! What were you thinking? Or were you thinking at all? I'm surprised the kids Mom didn't try to have you arrested or even murdered for that!"

"Hey, I was right there ready to help out. I guess the little guy was too much to handle and I helped slow him down," Zoe took a sip of her herbal tea while she chuckled to herself. "Oh well, the really bad thing was that I was too late, Macy's was sold out of the shoes I wanted," Zoe was the stereotypical single young woman, spending most of her time outside of work helping the local economy, so to speak. She liked looking glamorous and keeping up with the ever changing fashion trends, but she wasn't really without a heart.

"Always with the shoes. I'm surprised no one else was hurt on your way there," Emily pushed her bangs out of the way, and noticed someone coming over to her out of the corner of her eye.

"Muffins anyone?" She was hoping the food they ordered was finally being brought to them. The sky was turning dark and they all wanted to be long gone before the rain began again.

"Why hello there ladies, looks like a nice day, mind if I join you?" The voice sounded familiar, and not like one of the servers they knew so well from the years of coming here either. The man pulled a chair over from an adjacent table and sat down. Emily frowned at the sight of the face.

"Hello "Bob," how are you doing?" She asked

with only a hint of sarcasm, trying hard not to betray her true feelings.

"Well I'm doing just fantastic. The sun is shining for the moment, and the world is getting better minute by minute. Well, anyone want anything from inside?"

"I think we're good, thanks,"
"Alright then, I'll be back! Save a seat?" "Bob" disappeared into the coffee shop, and the ladies immediately looked at Emily for an explanation.

"He's a sort of friend of my husbands, I guess they served together or something. I'm not really sure though, his story is really sketchy," Zoe and the others were very interested.

"Do tell!"

"Like I said, I don't know anymore than anyone else. He says his name is "Bob," but I'm not sure he's telling the truth,"

"Oh fine, party pooper, we know you know more than you're letting on. Oh! Shhh!" "Bob" walked outside again, coffee and those mysteriously misplaced muffins in hand.

"Thought you ladies could use a little something to eat, how about some blueberry muffins? You know, with the integration of the worlds economy, the price of goods has dropped surprisingly low. Can you believe all four of these were only four dollars?"

"Wow, that's amazing, thank you for that little tidbit of knowledge, I feel better educated on the affairs of the world now," This time, Emily's sarcasm couldn't be contained. "Bob" was so obviously fake in his every gesture, word, and piece of clothing. It smelled so much like deception that she couldn't help but be pessimistic about his offer. But she still had to consider it. Her boss wouldn't recommend something if there wasn't at least a modicum of truth behind it. Isn't life, however it's lived, better than death? The thought was difficult to deal with at the moment, so Emily went back to drinking her tea and trying very hard not to choke "Bob," Emily isn't violent at all, but this character spewing forth garbage in front of her just happens to bring out strange primal urges locked deep inside of her. She wasn't really listening, but noticed he always seemed to have a crooked smirk on his face while telling stories, which are most likely tall tales, completely devoid of any truth anyway.

"So there I was, being chased by a Snow Leopard at the base of Mt. Everest! I dropped everything and just ran like the dickens, hoping to high hell I could outrun the son of a bitch. Turns out all it wanted was the bland food I was carrying in my pack! What a day though, spent five days and nights walking back to the settlement,"

"Oh, how nice, such a great story. Do you have any more adventures to share?"

"Why yes I do. But I think this story should only be heard by your ears. If you'll excuse us ladies, I think Emily and I will take a little walk," They said their goodbyes and then Emily and "Bob" set off down the sidewalk, coffee in hand, to have the conversation she had been dreading. They walked slowly towards the downtown area, the Max train zooming by as they stopped at an intersection. The weather had begun turning for the worse. The clouds overhead were an ominous dark grey color, blocking out the Sun almost completely, as if a metaphor for how Emily felt, all light and hope from her life held at bay by this strange man before her. They made their way across the intersection towards 3rd avenue as the rain started to fall. "I suppose you know this story already, though I'm not sure of how it ends. Maybe you can help me out with the ending?"

"I'm not so sure that I'm ready to commit to any decision just yet. I've just barely gotten over the fact that he's gone,"

"He doesn't have to be gone, well dead at least. Listen, what if I tell you he can come home after a certain number of years and spend his last days with his family. You know, retire like any other regular joe?"

"How do I know you're telling the truth?" Emily stopped in the middle of the sidewalk. The wind was starting to pick up, blowing her hair about wildly as she stared through the buildings beyond her field of vision. Frozen in time as she remembers how she and Allen used to sit by the window on rainy days like today, with coffee in hand as the rain provides a soothing background noise. "How do I know I'll ever actually get to see him again? How do I know this isn't some kind of goddamn dream concocted by you guys?" She finally looked back at "Bob" as she swept her wet bangs out of the way of her eyes. "Bob" stood there, smiling ear to ear, showing his yellowed teeth while he chuckled to himself quietly.

"Well that's just it isn't it? You can't really trust anything these days. Can't really trust anyone ever. How can anyone ever be sure of anything, except death. But life rarely ever offers this kind of opportunity, an opportunity at a second chance, to live again, to live for you and your child–"

"How do you know about that?" Emily's face betrayed her surprise at what he last said. No one except Allen knew about their child. Even close friends and old war buddies were kept from knowing. Hell, they had only found out a few days before the event that she hasn't even had time to go to her first Doctors visit to actually confirm it.

"I have my ways. If there is something to know, I know it," He stared into her eyes as he said it, rain dripping down his forehead and into his eyes, to which he didn't even blink. Accepting the fact that she'll never really know how he knows, she let it go. The world was a strange place, and with the evolution of technology and people like "Bob," anything was possible.

"So, are you ready to help the globe find itself again, to make history and stop history from repeating itself?" Emily continued to stare off into the distance, tears forming at the corner of her eyes.

"We can take whatever we please, and could easily make Allen our pawn against your will. But this is the dawning of a new age, and the world government doesn't do things like that anymore, so I'm here to ask very nicely if you'll help support the future of your world. Your child would benefit greatly from it. We'll even make sure you and your future daughter are set financially for the rest of your lives. Health insurance, money for college, every bill paid for. For the rest of your life. And I wasn't kidding about letting Allen retire with you, that's part of the deal,"

"Is this all in writing?" Emily said while fighting

back sobs.

"Every last bit. There'll be a contract for you to sign with all of the agreed upon terms. You can eve get a lawyer should we go back on our word. See how nice this new government is these days? You can even sue for secret stuff now!"

Without saying anything, Emily pulled a pen and piece of paper from her purse and wrote something on it, then she handed it to "Bob" and walked away, with tears trickling down her cheek. "Bob" stood there perplexed. He looked down at the small yellow note he had in his hand and slowly unfolded it. The rain smeared the ink, but it was still legible. "Huh, I guess this'll do," 1 O'clock, three days from now, Red Sunset Park. Bring contract.

* * * * *

Allen was lying on the ground, staring into the darkness above, trying to see the ceiling of the cave, still thinking about the comments from the day before. Sleep hadn't quite been the reprieve he had hoped, even though he wasn't expecting it to be. It felt like morning, although there was nothing to indicate that other than the bodies natural circadian rhythm beckoning him to wake up, even though he was awake most of the night. Mike was still sleeping soundly across the clearing, snoring away as if he were at home in his own bed. This could still be a nightmare.

He thought to himself, hoping it was just a strangely long nightmare. He had read about how time was distorted in dreams, with short events sometimes taking four real hours to occur, and long events only taking a few actual seconds to play out. So the possibility was still there. His eyes were dry and reddened from crying, and his mind numb from trying to figure everything out. His thoughts were interrupted by his stomach rumbling loud enough to wake up Mike and half the jungle.

"Way to ruin the night there pal," Mike yelled across the clearing, still laying down.

"Heh, sorry, don't remember when my last meal was," Come to think of it, Allen couldn't recall eating since he'd woken up here, making it at least three days or more.

"So what's on the breakfast menu for today?" Anything would be better than nothing at this point, even eating dirt.

Sitting up on his elbows, Mike scanned the jungle with his eyes and ears for signs of a possible food source. The jungle responded with eerie silence, except for the relaxing buzzing and chirping of insects hidden in the distance. Perplexed, Mike scratched his head and lied back down.

"Your guess is as good as mine. I'm not even

sure anything here is edible, let alone palpable for our delicate palates. Besides, in a few minutes we should try to find the exit from this cave, I'm pretty sure the answers we're looking for aren't down here. Even though we're having so much fun here,"

"Yeah, hey, what you were saying last night, are those things all true?"

"Well, sort of. I mean, the only thing I'm sure of is the fact that this isn't Earth. I mean, it's pretty obvious. The other stuff though? Who knows. This place could all be a hologram set up by the 'man,' or a twisted television show for psychotic children. Hell, it could be just a figment of your or my imagination,"

"Could this maybe be a nightmare?"

"Maybe, anything at all is possible. Either way, I'm here, you're here, where ever here is, so we might as well make the best of it, make our families proud and get home safely,"

"Make lemons out of lemonade?" That idiom was far overused, and probably not appropriate for this particular situation, there were no lemons to be had after all.

"Might be right though, but why would anyone want to abduct us? I still don't remember a damn thing, but what I do know is that humans aren't really terribly interesting prey," Allen sat up slowly, scooting back to rest his back on the log laying behind him.

"I mean, just look at us, nasty little creatures we are," He clasped his hands together thoughtfully, wondering if he has a family of his own somewhere, or if anyone at all is missing him right now. Maybe no one noticed, or no one cared so that he just faded away into oblivion, never to be heard from or seen again.

Not that it would matter, the way he felt at the moment he doesn't think anyone could possibly have cared anyway.

"Hey, you ok over there?" Mike was looking thoughtfully at him, one eyebrow up, probably trying to read his thoughts or something.

"Yeah, just reflecting on the finer things in life, like pants, and clean water and such,"

"Alright smart ass, your pants look just fine anyway, and who needs clean water when we can clean it ourselves? Am I right?" With that, Allen laughed, but only lightly. Time was of the essence here, or at least so they thought. If they were going to get out of here, they had better keep moving. The question that was on both of their minds was exactly where do they go next?

Mike stood up and walked towards the jungle, found what he was looking for and made a loud grunting noise and quite the show pulling it from the ground. He returned to their sleeping area with a five foot long stalk of a plant with furry orange fronds poking from out of it from the base to the tip. They were lightly swaying in the light breeze, or maybe they were moving of their own accord, Allen couldn't be sure. He set it down on a rock and started to pull on some loose strands on the frayed bottom of his left pant leg. With another dramatic show, and a hard fall onto the ground below him, Mike freed a strip of fabric and wrapped it around the plant.

"Mike, wait, you hear that?" Off in the distance Allen heard the faint snap of foliage. They were, presumably, alone, and any animals out in the jungle hadn't been careless enough to ruin their own environment, so it had to be something else.

"Hurry up man, I've got a bad feeling about this," Out of the corner of Allen's eye was a small flash of motion, just barely perceptible to the human eye, and then Mike leapt into action, striking a small stone against another stone stuck into the ground, showering the makeshift torch with sparks, put for some reason those sparks didn't seem to want to last. A breeze picked up with the wind flowing over their mussed hair. Both Allen and Mike looked over their shoulders, heard the guttural screams of the creatures. They looked at each other with worry behind their eyes and exclaimed at the same time, "Shit!"

FIGHT OR FLIGHT

The light was dim as he ran, jumping, hopping and leaping over vegetation that seemed to attack him as he went. A cool breeze tousled his grimy hair, pulled it in the direction that just might become freedom, or into something that might be the end of it all. His breathing came in fitful wheezes as he ran, his lungs burning from the exertion. One foot, then the other, in rapid succession. Jump over this root, run, fast, turn left to avoid the wall of the cavern, no exit there. Continue running, running for what seems like an eternity. The glowing creatures on the wall weren't glowing anymore, failing to light the way. The only light was coming from a makeshift torch somewhere behind him, but it was fading fast. Allen kept running as fast as he could, jinking and juking around the trees trying to capture him, looking for a way out of this mess.

Nothing made sense, everything was still a mystery, even his identity. He was taking this Mike's word for it, he did feel familiar and had no reason not to trust him. For now at least. There, up ahead, a small sliver of light appeared through the thick verdure. Salvation at last from at least this portion of Hell, or whatever it is. Just in time too, as he could smell the foul breath of the creatures following them. It was an absolute miracle that they were able to outpace them at all. Allen turned to look behind himself, carefully turning his head to see Mike running nearly as fast as he was, holding the homemade torch awkwardly in his right hand. Right behind Mike was the reptilian humanoid snarling as it chased behind them both. Up ahead the sliver of light was revealing itself to be what looked like an old entrance recently filled in with loose rubble.

"Jump!" Mike screamed behind him. "Jump now you idiot!" There was no need to be insulting, but that was the least of their issues. Allen continued on toward the light, seeming to pick up speed as he went, his heart pumping faster, his lungs working harder, burning more intensely. He was running so hard his extremities began to feel numb. Only twenty more feet to go, the light shining brighter and more intense with every hastened step. Allen protectively covered his face with his arm and stuck the other one out in front of him as he leapt towards the light, towards either a potential freedom or an oddly ironic death. But wouldn't death also bring the escape from this nightmare as well?

His arm bent slightly as he impacted the loose soil in front of his freedom. Curiosity strikes and Allen opens his eyes briefly but is blinded by the fierce blue sun that seemed to be glaring at him as if to warn him of some mysterious impending tragedy. As Allen squeezed his eyes shut to rid himself of the brilliant azure visage, his perception was inundated with manifestations of another reality, one that seemed so distant and unreal, yet so familiar. He could see the blurred outline of a man in a white lab coat, mouthing something frantically to him. His heart was beating hard, the vibrations could be felt throughout his body, and heard pulsating loudly in his ears. Before him, in the blurry visage, an arm, presumably his own, flailed wildly while the white coated figure tried to grab and control it. And just as fast as it appeared, the illusion disappeared, replaced by pain in the back of his skull and the bright sun ahead of him.

"Aaaghh!" Allen screamed as he fell for what seemed like eternity. He couldn't hear any activity behind him, and at this point he didn't really care too much. Allen landed on his feet with his knees bent, the force and relatively long distance caused his knees to buckle and roll a few feet to end up face down in the dry gritty soil at the edge of the overhang he dived onto. Dazed and confused Allen slowly brought his arms under him and lifted himself up, shaking his head to clear the fog that was creeping into his mind from the events of the fall. Before he even had a chance to stand-up, Mike vaulted out of the recently found opening at a high rate of speed, rolling and twisting in mid air only to land on his side and almost slide completely off of the ledge.

After a few seconds the dust finally settled and a shaky Mike attempted to stand up. The fall wasn't the issue, in fact the fall could almost be described as "fun" if it were anywhere else. It was just the botched and rather sudden landing that did it. Mike tried to hide a grimace of pain behind a crooked smile as he brought his legs under him and attempted to stand up. The heat from the blast itself could still be felt from above, buffeting him with a nice warm stream of air that gently brushed his grungy hair out from over his eyes. The blast of air was in stark contrast to the frigid and desiccant air outside. Allen was standing already, staring out into the distant landscape, seemingly frozen in time and space. His chest was barely rising and falling as he stood there with that cold dead look on his face. Mike chanced a look back at the crude opening above their heads, and only barely missed a shadowy brown blur spring forth ever so swiftly in a dive from the smoking vent towards the ledge below.

It happened too fast for Mike to do anything,

in mere milliseconds the creature was a shooting fireball careening towards Allen, and before he could blink, before he could even so much as let loose any kind of warning, the creature hit Allen, still on fire, with the agility of a feline, having reached one large clawed hand out to deftly grab Allen by the neck as it flew past. They flew towards the ground below, with Allen loosing only a small yelp as they fell into the darkness below. The unsightly creature landed on its back, with Allen's momentum carrying them both into a roll that stretched out for a few meters before the grotesque beast ended on top, poised over him with the other enormous clawed appendage held high in the air, the polished osseous protrusions for claws catching the light of the cerulean star as it rose over the horizon. This was quite possibly the last moment of Allen's life, staring into the large eyes of a saurian beast that seemed utterly surreal.

Instinct seemed to grab ahold as Allen's limp arms sprang into action and came up to try to resist the herculean strength attempting to squeeze the life out of him. The beasts eyes lit up with what appeared to be an imitation of glee as he bared his fangs. The powerful beast was just too much for the meager strength Allen still had. The razor sharp claw was inching ever more closely as the seconds ticked slowly by, seeming as if they were hours instead. In the face of death, Allen stared deep into the creatures eyes, into it's very soul as it stared back snarling and drooling. Allen didn't see anger in it's eyes though, but instead saw something else entirely, a scene maybe, of something far away yet so familiar.

Mike was already on the ground, running as fast as his tired legs could take him. He nearly flew over the ground as he went, staring intently at his target, praying he wouldn't notice before too long. Fifty yards passed faster than a blink of a eye, and leaped towards his quarry violently, and closed his eyes, hoping he wasn't too late.

* * * * *

Suddenly there was an overwhelming feeling of relief that washed over Allen as something heavy, again, fell from his chest. He hardly noticed as he was practically in a daze still stuck on the glimpse of... something that was so vivid in the eyes of the beast. The fuck. Mike!
"Mike!" He screamed.

A mere three feet or so away was a dusty human figure rolling through the landscape like a tumbleweed, fighting for dominance with the ferocity of animals vying for territory. When the dust settled, a heavily sweating Mike was mounted on top using his weight and every ounce of strength to trap the arms and hold it down.

"ALLEN!" Mike screamed, his voice straining

under the effort to keep his life. "ALLE..!" His scream was cut short as his face was pelted with the slimy sputum of his attacker.

Luckily, Allen was closing in as fast as he could, only losing his balance once along the way. Mike took a position above the creatures head, still curious about the phenomena he experienced when he gazed into the eyes of the beast. In fact, Allen wanted to experience that again, it seemed so familiar and so right. Even with it struggling with Mike, it still stared deep into his eyes again. There it is! That's it, I can feel it, that's...

"ALLEN! FUCKIN.. KILL IT! JUST KILL IT!"

Allen's reverie was broken by the agonizing plea to end their predicament. No matter, whatever it was that Allen was about to comprehend was lost as soon as he came to. After shaking his head to clear his mind, his eyes immediately fell onto a rock laying just a few inches away. Without hesitation he picked up the rock, just small enough to fit in one hand, and slammed it down as hard as possible on the snarling visage below, not once, but again and again until the cold blue blood stopped flying from what remained of the head.

"Nice one! Looks like they die just like anything else, that's a relief,"

Allen wasn't quite as excited as Mike was, and only vaguely smiled up at him as he sat down in the tacky, now blueish, dirt. A thousand different things were flying through his head at the moment, not the least how easily their attacker was subdued. Just what the hell was that that he saw? He could hardly remember what it was, and could only recall that there was indeed something, something that was vaguely familiar shining brightly through those dark reptilian eyes.

"Hey man listen, it's over, and we have to get out of here. If we wait any longer, there may be many more of those damn things coming after us. Especially now that we've killed one of them, they'll want revenge,"

Mike had a more serious demeanor about him than usual as he said it, but Allen still just sat there, too weak to move after the ordeal. And still very confused over what he had just seen. Dammit! If only life were a little easier than this bullshit.

"Listen, I know, it's tough having to kill anything, even if it is trying to kill you too, but we can talk about that after we remove ourselves from this death wish of an open area,"

"It's not that, it's... something else. I can't really explain it, but I had a feeling of familiarity or something, like the beast was a part of me, or at the very least we were connected in some way. I'm not really sure though,"

"I hate to break it to you, but we can definitely talk about it as soon as we find some shelter. You can even cry on my shoulder if you'd like," Even though Mike was only trying to ease the tension, it wasn't really working. Either way, Allen finally realized the danger they could potentially be in if they stayed where they were and slowly rose to his feet, his muscles aching.

"What the fuck Mike, What the fuck are we supposed to do now? We have no god dammed idea where we are, no fucking clue where to go, and no idea if there is any hope of getting out of this bloody hell hole anyway!" Allen was furious at this point. They had been here for an unknown, yet relatively long, amount of time and he wasn't about to just wander the desert blindly without some semblance of God dammed direction.

"I don't even remember my name, and I'm only trusting you blindly because you seem just a little bit familiar. I still don't know who the fuck you are!" Allen's arms were out in front of him as if he were crushing the blue star itself.

"What do you want from me Allen? Huh, what exactly do you want me to say to you? Do you want me to wave my magic wand, say a couple of words and magically make us appear back on

Earth? Well that's fucking absurd. Following that things foot prints is likely the only way we'll be able to live at all. Or at least die an honorable death instead of from dehydration and heat exhaustion. At least I'm trying to fucking do something here, any better ideas?"

"You still didn't answer my last question, and no. It just doesn't seem worth it to me, doesn't seem worth the risk. Hell, we could eek out a meager existence in that cave up there, hole up for the rest of our lives and live peacefully as opposed to what the fuck ever you want to go do," Allen, or whoever he was at this point, seemed to have lost the will to fight, the will to survive. His brain was filled with jumbled thoughts racing in and out of his consciousness that made absolutely no sense, they were making him light headed most of the time. He felt that his own thoughts weren't even his own, that there was no purpose in this little game. Allen had lost it, he had nothing, he was nothing, there was no reason for him to continue on this fucked up journey through who knows where and for what exactly? Allen's hands and arms finally fell to his side, limp from exhaustion, and he collapsed to sit on a mound of sand and dirt below him. He stared off into the distance, away from seemingly everything. His eyes turned glassy and his expression blank, as if he had perished right where he sat.

"So go have your God dammed fun and get the

hell out of here. By yourself, I don't want to go because my idea seems a hell of a lot better than anything you've said so far," Mike didn't skip a beat, and deflected Allen's ultimatum as soon as he opened his mouth. He sat down next to him, and slowly put his hand on Allen's shoulder. The atmosphere was surprisingly calm considering the recent events that transpired, though Allen flinched at the touch.

"Listen, I know you still don't believe me, I can feel it, and I can certainly here it in your voice, but just listen for a minute, okay? I didn't think in the slightest that you'd just take my word at face value back there. I counted on you doubting me, that's just like the Allen I remember! But listen, that familiar feeling you have is because we share a deep bond, a bond that's been forged through the fires of battle. We've done such wonderful and such horrible things together, and we've watched many friends and even nations die at the hands of some terrible people. Deep down inside I know you, my friend Allen, are still there, regardless of what's going on in that noggin of yours right now. And like always, I'm going get you and me home safe. It's the least I can do for you," Allen's body was still limp, yet rigid. His gaze still fixated on the beyond. Mike wondered what Allen saw, if he was looking at something inward, or outward?

"You don't have to follow me, you can go about your business if you want to. But you do have a family at home, a wife and an unborn child that need you. I know you probably don't believe me, and I don't expect it. But I know that they wouldn't want to disappoint them. They would want you to come home to them, regardless of whether or not you remember who they are or not. Hell, I don't want you to disappoint them!" For Allen, it was different. The thought of being completely lost, of forgetting himself seemingly so easily. If it was this easy to forget who he was, then wouldn't it be equally as easy for anyone that knew him to just forget him? What really was the point, then, of going back to a family that has most likely already forgotten he ever existed? What was the point of trying to rebuild a life completely, almost from the beginning? The thought of never being able to be himself again, of forever knowing that something is and always will be missing was all very daunting. Even if he did have a wife and a child somewhere out there, did it really matter at this point? He was so far gone from whomever we was before that life simply wouldn't be the same anyway, and was that in any way fair to his could be family?

This was an existential crisis of nearly epic proportions. It's almost as if the entity that he was, was a mere manifestation of something else, a false persona, a false reality in a way. The implications were making Allen nauseous so he hunched over holding his stomach, hoping to keep its contents inside.

"I don't think you understand Mike, I just don't think you get it. Try putting yourself in my shoes for a minute, try reversing the roles here and tell me how you would feel about everything that's happened so far," Mike was looking blankly into Allen's eyes as he said this, almost as if he were bored.

"All I'm saying is that regardless of what you say to me, I still don't believe it. I don't have that capacity, literally. This is all some magical dream and I feel like I was just born. I've got glimpses of something flashing through my faulty brain, but I STILL CAN'T TRUST ANYTHING YOU SAY!"

The wind had started to pick up again, making a mockery of their vision. But off in the distance, away from the cliff face they emerged from, was an indentation in the ground, something distinct, although still quite difficult to see.

"Hey, Allen, look over there," Mike pointed at the impression in the dirt, which was slowly fading as the sand storm was picking up speed.

"What? I don't see anything but swirling wind and sand in my eyes," Allen tried squinting his eyes to protect them from the fine grained ocular intruders in an effort to increase his visual acuity. But all he could see was sand and even more sand that seemed to go on forever in the expanse before them.

"I think that's the footprint of this guys little friend, or maybe not, I... Wait, yeah! That's definitely a footprint, and theres more over here!," Allen walked over to where Mike was investigating his lead.

"I don't think the other one got away, did it? This doesn't really make sense, and I don't think we should follow something that wants to kill us," Allen was just trying to use common sense. What intelligent being would make their escape, if it even did escape, so obvious unless it was a trap?

"Easy now big fella, I'm sure it is a trap, but in any case it'll probably lead us to something useful, like water, food and shelter," Mike looked oddly calm as he gave his reasons, as if he could predict the future and saw them calmly walking ever so silently into the promised land unscathed. "Besides, it'll be better if we spring the trap on our terms anyway," He was right, regardless of whether they walked into a trap by following these footprints, these creatures would inevitably hunt them down wherever they went.
"I've got a bad feeling about this!"

HOPE

They had been walking for what seemed like forever, and seeing as they had no point of reference for time or otherwise, it made the journey feel even longer. The dust storm was at its peak and was starting to wind down, though it had taken its toll on the lone travelers, buffeting their skin like so many sharp needles. In such conditions it was nigh impossible to actually effectively track anything, much less shallow imprints embedded in a sandy surface. The footprints they were trying to follow had disappeared what seemed to be a long time ago and they were merely wandering blindly through the sandstorm along a long flat expanse that seemed to lead to nowhere. For all they knew, they had been walking in circles. So much for a trap, unless this was it, trapping them in the madness of their own minds.

As the sandstorm finally whirled to a close, burning off the last of it's fierce energy, the bright sapphire high up in the sky was also nearing the end of tour, leaving nothing but emptiness, a starless sky that nearly blanketed everything in darkness. Everything except a small speckle of bright white light far off in the distance, in the direction they just so happened to be heading.

"Holy shit, Allen, do you see that?"

"I never thought we'd actually find anything but death in this desert,"

"I was beginning to think the same. So what's the plan? We definitely shouldn't be running in there with our testosterone flying, there's no telling what's lurking in there," Mike, again, was right. There was no use running into something unprepared, and Mike originally wanted to spring a devious trap on their terms anyway.

"There's no cover, at all, from here all the way to that light source, so we'll have to move as far to the outside as possible, keeping a low profile. Me thinks they can smell a bit better than us, and that they can probably see in the dark, at least that's what cheap horror movies tell me, so let's be silent and swift," The light may be to their advantage, effectively rendering potential sensitive eyesight useless, but it also is a huge disadvantage, silhouetting them against the dark nothingness beyond them. They might as well stroll in casually whistling a happy tune.

After rubbing the gritty sand all over their

exposed skin and clothes they set off silently under the cover of darkness towards the light. Allen thought it strange that they were walking towards the light when that's a common euphemism for dying, almost fitting for their situation. Mike took point, walking slowly and carefully so as not to disturb the landscape too much. Allen was about eight meters back and four meters to Mikes right, walking just as slowly and carefully and taking a wide arc to the outside, trying their damnedest to look like weeds on the wind, or perhaps a part of a new storm system throwing sand about.

Perhaps it was the constant threat of being spotted as they were practically silhouetted against the abyss of a night from the lights illuminating the perimeter ahead combined with the deliberate and cautious pace they were keeping, but forever took on an even more fresh meaning.

As they neared the light, the details of the structures slowly began to emerge. The light was coming from a single slender light post that seemed to be at the center of a temporary encampment consisting of half a dozen metallic domelike structures in a semi-circle that backed to the base of a range of rather steep yet petite hills. There didn't seem to be any activity at all happening in the encampment, in fact it seemed abandoned. The light, then, must be automatic and perhaps solar powered, or it was recently abandoned. Regardless, their pace remained painstakingly slow and steady if indeed there were any surprises to be had.

Mike and Allen ran the last hundred meters or so to the edge of the outermost building, a domed prefabbed metal structure that seemed to be suited for Humans rather than Kasai. They both kneeled down next to the outermost edge, a few meters a part from each other. Mike took his time peering around the corner at the center of the semi-circular camp. There was a flag pole, but no flag, and more perimeter lights shining ever so brightly towards the interior. Which was odd, considering any threats on a foreign land would most likely be from outside and highlighting their own assets would almost certainly mean an unavoidable doom, which is probably why it was empty anyway.

Allen tapped Mike on the shoulder and they rounded the opposite side of the structure to find the entrance. The door was half gone, with the shattered remains hanging loosely from the hinges on the left side. The size of the door was another good indication that this was a Human settlement and f this was indeed, then they were placing their lives into the cold hand of fate that they were at least somewhat friendly. Or even alive still. Silently, Mike crossed the threshold of the doorway, pushing aside the broken remnants of the door, thank God it didn't make a noise, and entered with practiced speed and efficiency from years of supposedly working together. Allen followed close behind, instinctively taking up a position at the left side of the structure as Mike stopped short on the right side.

"Jesus," Mike whispered. The lights outside cast a grim almost unreal quality to the scene before them. The floor was littered with test equipment, technology and furniture. All covered in dust making it seem as if it were a crypt that hasn't been touched by anyone for hundreds of years. The air was ripe with the sweet stench of stale food and mold. Most shocking of all was the dark stains that streaked the walls and deritus like someone was painting. If that was blood, there were no bodies or even any remains to be seen. The lights still on outside meant it couldn't have been too long since whatever this was happened. So where was the evidence of a massacre? Not even a bloodied finger to be found. Whatever had happened here had happened in a moment of pure savage indignation.

Out of instinct more than anything, Allen started carefully walking the perimeter of the structure, looking for any evidence to suggest what had caused the atrocity before them. That and he was scouring for any communication equipment that might help them on their quest to get the hell out of here. It was unlike an expedition of any kind to not have an emergency beacon or distress signal. There was a host of scientific equipment, mostly biological in nature. Large now cracked screens hanging by their power cords swinging back and forth over a transparent cylinder that was still full of a course limpid liquid. Just beyond that Allen caught a glint of flashing metal in his eye, what looked like a ring around greying flesh of a hand that was connected to something buried under a desk.

"Mike, get over here, fast," Allen's heart races as he tries without success to move a prefabbed plastic desk off of a half decomposed corpse. A half decomposed human corpse.

"That's definitely human, has to be. Married even. What do you think happened here?" Mike scratched his head, confused as ever at what they found.

"I'm not sure, but judging by the equipment littering the floor, I'd say this is a scientific expedition of some sort," Without saying another word Mike bend down to help lift the desk off the victim. His face was half gone, ripped from his skull, the other half barely hanging by what little muscle and sinew that remained. What a horrible way to die. Mike was the first to break the uncomfortable silence that followed.

"Looks like the Kasai had come through here. Probably just senseless murder, another unfortunate trait of their species," It was clear that Mike had little regard for the sentient beings of this planet, but there was clearly a story being told here that was more than just a blood thirsty rampage.

"Hey Mike, what is this?" Allen was confused, and thought that they were the only humans on this rock, according to Mike at least.

"I have no idea buddy, I had no idea that this was here, nor do I have any idea what the fuck they were doing man," Mike stared at the corpse, his nose wrinkled in disgust. "But I'm sure they were just minding their own business, not even bothering those things at all. No one deserves anything like this, I don't care who you are," Mike was right. Despite the multitude of activities that could have been happening, invasive, destructive or otherwise, no one deserved a cruel death.

"In your honest opinion, no bullshit, what do you think we're doing here?" It was hard to keep their voices quiet now, given how fresh the carnage was the Kasai were probably long gone by now.

"Probably a medical facility, to either bring aid or to help some explorers,"
"Okay, so how the fuck did you get here Mike. I may be amnesic, but I'm not stupid, you've been lying to me and this settlement is more proof of that. So just how the fuck did you get

here, and what the fuck are you doing here," Allen's tone was creeping towards angry, and raising quickly in volume. There were a lot of unanswered questions he wanted from this "Mike" character, and a lot of things just weren't adding up. Allen's stare intensified.

"Alright, before you go all apeshit on me, you're right, I have been lying to you, but only to protect you. I was sent here to see what went wrong at this research outpost. We've lost contact a few months ago, but were unable to send any help out here until the jokers on the committee in congress could stop squabbling for a few seconds to actually make a god dammed decision for once," Mike was shaking at this point, and sat down on the just moved desk, a pop was heard as his weight settled on the desk, no doubt dislocating a joint of another victim of this mess.

"And look, I really don't know what happened to you, okay? You weren't part of my team, they all didn't even survive the few minutes after we landed, we were ambushed," Mike's gaze fell down towards the motionless decomposing remnants of this building, staring beyond as if there was something there on another level.

"Our ship was destroyed shortly after, and then I found you in the cave. That's it, I swear, now if we want to find another way out of here, alive, then lets put all this crap aside, okay?"

Mike was still staring through the ground, moisture beginning to appear at the corners of his eyes.

"Fine, but you have to promise me that you'll at least try to keep the same story. And make it believable at lea..." His comment trailed off as a stabbing pain erupted from the back of his head pulsating to the rhythm of his heart. To Allen, it seemed as if thousands of tiny hypodermic needles were simultaneously injecting and drawing in to the tune of his life's force. The pain was familiar, very familiar, having happened what seemed like days ago when he first arrived. It made him weak in the knees, so he slowly collapsed to the floor, barely missing the jagged broken edge of the remains of a metal desk that was nearby. Mike didn't even have a chance to react it all happened so quickly. A bright flash flared searing pain into Allen's eyes as he went down, persisting and blinding him. Mike stood, mouth a gape, unsure of what to do.

"Allen? Buddy, this isn't a good time to be doing this, we need to keep alert to stay alive. Come on now! Don't freaking do this!"

In the background Allen heard only a deafening high frequency hum that further disoriented him. His senses were being barraged with stimuli, even his tactile senses were numb from searing throbbing pain. Hidden in the intense background ringing was something else, though Allen wasn't nearly aware enough to discern exactly what it was, but it was a mix of sounds that were themselves familiar, a collection of frequencies that had a meaning that resonated deep within, with almost angelic qualities. Allen struggled to remain conscious enough to listen, and suddenly realized that what he was hearing were voices. And then the realization slowly came to the forefront of his mind that he had heard these before, at least one of them. It sounded like a woman, a gorgeous woman, whispering and conveying comforting thoughts and words of encouragement.

Telling me to hold on. A beautiful sight flashed before his eyes, soft feminine features and long dirty blond hair connected to the most beautiful woman he had ever seen. He gasped and sat up suddenly, his heart was beating fast and hard enough to cause tremors as raised his lower back and reach a shaky arm towards the woman. And then it all vanished, almost as fast as it had appeared. Allen lied in a pool of his own sweat and drool mixed with hundred year old dust and dirt, shivering from the freezing temperature. Hadn't it just been nearly a hundred degrees?

It was still dark, Allen had his eyes closed, squeezing them shut so as to prevent even the slightest sliver of light from disturbing the peacefulness he was feeling. Above him he had an inkling that someone was standing over him, watching him intently, though not saying anything. The pain was gone though, for now. So that was at least one positive aspect Allen could think of. The man above shifted his weight and finally spoke, though Allen and an inkling he was going to say something.

"Yo, bro, are you okay? That was a mighty spill you took. Are you bleeding?"

Allen stirred, slowly turning around to his back so he could properly sit up. Back to reality now, the dream is over.

"I think I'm alright, no major damage here," He grinned, barring his teeth in a display of mock confidence. External damage was a non issue, and completely nonexistent anyway, it was the internal damage that was so clear yet mysterious that mattered, but what could Mike do about that anyway?

"So, I think it'd be a good idea to get some rest now, maybe make camp here and continue on in the morning. If the Kasai were indeed here, they are long gone and this place is in the back of their minds, so we should be okay for now. Regardless, I'll take first watch, for a few hours then you can suffer some more. Sound good?" As Mike said this, he was looking around for something suitable to use as bedding material. A broken desk, some broken chairs and a dirty floor were all that could be found in the immediate vicinity. Allen got to his knees and breathed in deeply, taking his time to fully get up, if at all.

Mike saw a locker by the door that had been un-tampered with, so he strolled over casually and took the bright red plus sign to mean there might be something potentially useful in it. Thankfully it was unlocked, so nothing else had to suffer any damage today.

"Hey, I think there's an emergency blanket in here, at least there should be. Hey! Don't get up man, just lie your ass back down and relax, I'll bring this stuff to ya,"

Mike grabbed two emergency blankets and used one to cover Allen where he lay, and the other to use as a pillow for the sensitive head of Allen's.

"Just relax buddy, we can do some more exploring after a few hours rest. It's been a long day. I'll wake you up in a few," As Mike said that, Allen slowly drifted off into blissful sleep. The stress of the day had taken its toll on him.

NIGH

The night went quickly, without much in the way of dreams. Allen didn't really dream anymore, it seems that once he awoke on this forsaken planet that all the joy of life, including the simple escape from reality that is dreaming, was taken from him. Allen stirred slowly, taking his time to wake fully. It had been awhile since he had even so much as shut his eyes for a brief period, so every second was savored as if it were his last.

"Hey Mike," Allen kept his eyes closed as he made sure his companion was still alive. "Mike, wake up, I think it's morning now, time to wake up and smell the roses" But Mike was no where to be found. Allen tried to sit up, but thick twine was wrapped tightly around his wrists, leaving indentations in his skin. Allen rolled slowly onto his back, finding his hands resting on the cold metal of a lock that helped the twine keep freedom at bay.

"This isn't funny Mike, get out here and untie me, we have a long day ahead of us," His angered voice fell on no one. Straining his neck to look around, Allen noticed that he was no longer in the building he had fallen asleep in, but was sitting awkwardly on dirt floor, at the bottom of a sizable pit, at least two average humans in depth. Being here in this foreign land was a nightmare. Being shackled and trapped has transformed his nightmare into a night terror. It was as if he had just woken up for the first time in this hell hole.

"Mike! You bastard, this isn't fucking funny!" Allen struggled against the twine, but it was useless, the more he struggled the tighter it seemed to become, almost cutting off circulation to his hands. He rolled over, however, and stared up at the naked metal roofing above with grim determination in his eyes, attempting to make it crash down on top of him with the power of his will alone. Death would be a better fate than anything that might await him now.
It seemed as if several hours had passed by, hunger and thirst biting at him, when a quiet rustling noise approached the pit. The pain in the back of Allen's head began again, pulsating just below the surface of his consciousness almost to the rhythm of the approaching footsteps.

"I'm sorry about the accommodations, it was

the best we could find on such short notice," The familiar voice sounded cocky and pleased with himself as he spoke. Allen imagined a gruff half smile on his face as he spoke. Mike stood at the edge of the pit, peering down into Allen's eyes, a smile gleaming from ear to ear on his face. "My friend, we simply couldn't let you complete their so called prophecy and destroy an entire civilization. It would just be uncouth, So, you see, we had to neutralize you,"

"Who's w.." Allen was interrupted quickly.

"Myself and these beautiful people here," Mike interrupted gracefully.
"The Kasai had contacted me and asked if I could help them with a small issue. The stars were aligning, or whatever bullshit, so they needed a quick solution before it began. Why you were in their dream, or prophecy or whatever, I have no idea, but they identified you as the root of their problem,"

"I don't even know what or who these people are, so how the hell can I destroy an entire civilization. I'm supposedly in retirement according to you, so what kind of sense does that even make? You've been had you idiot, but whatever," Allen was mad, but surprisingly, he was keeping his calm. There was nothing that he could do anyway. Might as well go out the better man, he thought.

"On the contrary, my dear old friend, we've already apparently invaded their home world, killing hundreds of thousands of them for, for nothing. No strategic or material goal. Pure. Genocide. What the hell man, do you really think they're going to take this kind of thing lightly? Don't you think these people would take every measure feasible in order to prevent that? Don't you remember what we fought for? You don't do you. You don't remember a goddamned thing, and thats part of the problem. You have no idea what it was like watching the innocent suffer while we mindlessly pursued our useless and arbitrary goals to 'better humanity'. Do you know how many fucking thousands of children we had to see burn alive from 'strategic' forest fires. And this, someone getting the bright idea to invade these poor souls home, and why? Simply because we can? Because we want to be better? Because we want to live in the shadow of dictators past? You don't get it Allen, because you can't remember anything, because you can't see the eyes of the people we couldn't help, the people we had to leave to die on their own without us. Of all the sacrifices we made in vain,"Mike's gestures became more and more vivid and lively as the rant went on, his eyes burning with passion as he spoke.

"We've been doing this kind of thing for centuries Allen. Killing for ridiculous and frivolous reasons. Using the idea of a higher power, or the assumption of supremacy to justify the slaughter of millions. It's time to end that. Now. These people, the Kasai are a beautiful species. They've built so much, travelled far and wide among the stars, and they care, Allen. They look upon all life the same, with respect and reverence. War isn't even in their native vocabulary, conflicts have been solved with contests and through peaceful dialogue. They are so far evolved from us, that I'm surprised they even wasted their time seeking me out," Regardless of the why's and wherefores, or even how true his statements were, he believed every word he was saying, as if he were a messiah spreading the gospel of the deity of the moment. And he was becoming more and more resentful towards his own species. How could something like this happen? How could a once decent human being turn his back completely like this. There certainly must be other avenues of dealing with his anger. It seems so deep seated though, rooted deep in Mike's personality from years of abuse and neglect. Years of suffering.

"What the hell are you talking about man, I have nothing to do with that. And really? We can hardly send a probe to the other end of the solar system, let alone another fucking inhabited planet. I don't believe you, so go back to your precious friends and have them tell you the truth, because that isn't it,"
"Hell, We've been taking to the stars for a few years now. Mars and the Moon are colonized and we've been sending probes past our solar system

for years. Just last year an 'expedition' was sent out to search for life, but what they didn't know was that the actual mission was to destroy the Kasai, because they are a perceived threat to humanity. How can anyone condone genocide of an entire species! How can anyone do something so goddamn horrible!" The emotion in hims was rising with the amplitude of his voice, the tension in the air so tight it could be broken simply by breathing in the wrong direction.

"Mike, seriously, fucking stop this. You sound absolutely crazy. And you're not making any sense. I have nothing to do with any of that, I don't even know who I am for gods sake! How the hell could it be even remotely possible that I am actually connected or even fucking know what you are talking about!?"

"You're just like everyone else Allen, just as heartless and cold as anyone else of our species. But these people have awoken me to the greater possibilities that exist in the universe. These beautiful creatures have shown me just how amazing and precious life actually is. Don't you see? Don't you see the errors we've made throughout our lives, the trails of destruction we've left? And for what? For the 'greater good?' So that someone else's idea of whats right can be thrust onto the conquered?"

"Mike, fucking stop this, you're insane, you've gone ma..."

"QUIET! You shall not speak unless the great Kasai bid it! They are our masters now!" Mike had clearly lost his marbles at this point, almost near completely. Mike had been lost to some fanatical religion that has pushed his supposed close friend to the breaking point, crushing and controlling his mind for, what exactly? Genocide of his own species? Explanations and answers were still beyond hope. Par for the course.

Before Allen drifted in to the panicked throughs of isolation, Mike stared deeply into his eyes, into his very soul, and looked as if he were having second thoughts about his actions.

"I must establish a paradigm, and show these creatures that we are morally superior, just as they are. You are guilty of crimes beyond typical punishment, and for those heinous crimes you will be destroyed and flung back to Earth, mutilated beyond all recognition, bearing a message inside your chest cavity. It was your fathers expedition that began this atrocity, and so it will be fitting that it is now your destiny to end it,"

Allen closed his eyes and waited, breathing deeply while he attempted in vain to not worry about the coming end to his life. Funny isn't it? Dying a lonely soul, in a place that no one will ever find. But it didn't bother him as much as one might think. But the end didn't come. At least not this moment. Mike faded into the darkness beyond the pit, and with that an emptiness stung in Allen's mind, as if he could feel Mike's presence removing itself. He kept his eyes closed, and lied there quietly waiting for the sweet embrace of sleep, if it were to come at all.

LIFE

Emily sat beside his bed, holding his hand expectantly, willing him to wake. Willing this day to finally be over, and him alive once more. Hoping for success. As low a success rate as it was, she was confident in his will to survive. He had made it this far, after-all.

The life-support machine was near silent, blipping softly and slowly to indicate that there was life still within, though barely. The implantation of healthy stem cells was successful. At least his body hadn't rejected them outright. All they could do now, is wait. Wait for the impossible.

Emily had been sitting by his side for nearly three days, waiting, hoping, praying. "Come on baby, I believe in you. We need you, please work damn it, please…" She pleaded every day for life to be infused again within him. Three very long and very exhausting days.

"Uhh," Perhaps new life, at least, was going to enter this world today as Emily's water broke. She squeezed his hand lovingly, desperately. "I need you now more than ever Allen, please come back. Allen, it's time to wake up," With that, she called for a nurse and was escorted out of the room, ready to give new life into this world.

DREAMS

Alllennn. It's time to wake up. It's time to do what is necessary. The clock is ticking... Tick... Tock... Tick... Tock... Out of the darkness of his mind, a blinding light fills his vision, burning his very soul. He is disoriented, it could be three thousand years into the future, or it could very well be prehistoric Earth. The flash of light that seemed to last an eternity suddenly falls from his vision, fading once again to the black emptiness that is his mind. That voice, it's familiar yet so difficult to recognize and so completely out of place. His mind searching for recognition, the distinctive slow, morose raspy speech, awkward stress on syllables and unneeded pauses bringing absolutely no recollection. Come now Allen, we can't... wait, forever, now can, we? Time... is of... the essence. You have so much more to do, so much more to accomplish. The voice filled his whole being, reverberating across time and space as Allen stay motionless, listening, unable to speak or to act. It felt as if a great weight had been thrust upon his chest, crushing not only his body, but his soul. He struggled to breath, inhaling and exhaling laboriously. The voice chuckled slowly, almost sounding forced. There is no time for rest, the world needs you... Allen. The world needs you to act, to take matters into... your... own hands... Allen's seemingly floating, paralyzed body was bathed in light as pain once again erupted from the back of his head, warm blood dripping from his old wound, opened again, by what he didn't know. A vision flashed into his mind, a small child giggling, a woman sitting nearby. It faded as quickly as it appeared, replaced by blinding light and a face, a very familiar face staring into his eyes. Those beautiful blue eyes... And it too faded, only a forgotten memory from the depths of his soul. You aren't so lucky as to... just... die... Scam your... way... out of life. You... have suffered much... Have caused much suffering... but you are needed now... So wake up my dear friend. Off in the distance, as the sun rose and blinded him, Allen heard a distance and hollow click.

"Uhhh," His head was aching again. It was as if he had been sleeping on his back, with the back of his head lying on a bed of rusty, dull nails. Except Allen was lying face down again. In the same pit he was last time he was awake. Awake, as if it made a difference to be in any state other than dead at this point. Trapped and alone. Cold and injured. There was no reason to continue on. Except a nagging feeling in the back of his head, a voice so-to-speak urging him to continue on, to fight. To escape. Out of pure habit, he took his hands and put them by his sides so he could sit up, only this time the twin unwound itself and the cold, stiff lock fell to the dirt with a muffled thunk.

Tears streamed silently from his eyes, not out of sadness, or even joy, but more from confusion and dry eyes. It was indeed time for action. Time for Allen to once again become the man that he was and still is. Time to live.

Allen's breathing was slow and heavy, and the dull ache had returned to the back of his head. A soft almost artificial light bled through his eyelids. Slowly, Allen regained his sense of awareness. His arms were... to his side? The temperature was pleasant, as was the sweet floral aroma in the room. It was, once again, very... familiar. His eyes struggled to open, heavy from the burdens of the night, and crusted over from countless hours of sleep. The ambiance was also different, he noticed. There was... activity? Walking? A tile floor perhaps? At last, with the new ambiance and aroma filling his senses, Allen opened his eyes to the soft artificial light beyond. And the silhouette of a face he recognized, and never wanted to see again.

"Hello Allen, welcome back to the land of the living. I trust you had sweet dreams?"

ABOUT THE AUTHOR

JD Williams is an aspiring new author who is using his experiences in the Military as inspiration for stories. He's an avid reader of science fiction, specifically the Star Wars Extended Universe, and enjoys Japanese Martial Arts in his free time.

Our hero will return! This is only the beginning of a new era for our lone hero! What will happen next? Will he save the world and get the girl in the process? Will our untamed hero discover the secrets to the universe, unlocking pure evil in the process? Stay tuned to find out!

www.ingramcontent.com/pod-product-compliance
Lightning Source LLC
Chambersburg PA
CBHW030600130626
46552CB00006B/2608